Once Upon a Garden

Layla's Luck

Jo Rooks

MAGINATION PRESS 🍂 WASHINGTON, DC
American Psychological Association

For Ella, Michaiah, Sydney, and Zoe.
With love to Ruby and Xavi —*JR*

Books for Kids From the
American Psychological Association

Copyright © 2020 by Jo Rooks. Published in 2020 by Magination
Press, an imprint of the American Psychological Association.
All rights reserved. Except as permitted under the United States
Copyright Act of 1976, no part of this publication may be
reproduced or distributed in any form or by any means, or
stored in a database or retrieval system, without the prior
written permission of the publisher.

Magination Press is a registered trademark of the American
Psychological Association. Order books at maginationpress.org
or call 1-800-374-2721.

Book design by Gwen Grafft

Printed by Lake Book Manufacturing, Inc., Melrose Park, IL

Library of Congress Cataloging-in-Publication Data
Names: Rooks, Jo, author, illustrator.
Title: Layla's luck / by Jo Rooks.
Description: Washington, DC : Magination Press, 2020. | Series:
    [Once upon a garden] | "American Psychological Association." |
    Summary: "Layla is a very lucky ladybug. When she enters into
    a baking competition, she realizes she cannot always rely on her
    luck"— Provided by publisher.
Identifiers: LCCN 2019033989 | ISBN 9781433832383 (hardcover)
Subjects: CYAC: Luck—Fiction. | Baking—Fiction. | Contests—
    Fiction. | Friendship—Fiction. | Ladybugs—Fiction.
Classification: LCC PZ7.1.R66854 Lay 2020 | DDC [E]—dc23
LC record available at https://lccn.loc.gov/2019033989

Manufactured in the United States of America
10 9 8 7 6 5 4 3 2 1

This is Layla.

Ladybugs are known to be lucky,

and Layla thought she was very lucky indeed.

She had a lucky charm for every occasion!

Some lucky socks,

a lucky shamrock,

a lucky cup,

a lucky spoon,

a lucky pencil,

3

a lucky number,

and a lucky watering can.

When Layla won the race on sports day,
she thanked her **lucky** socks.

When she got a good grade on her spelling test,
she cheered her **lucky** pencil.

And when she grew the tallest flowers, she praised her **lucky** watering can.

One day, something very exciting
was happening in the garden.

William was looking up recipes.

Bella was finding ingredients.

And Eddie was
weighing them out.

Layla thought baking
looked very complicated.

Then she had an idea!

"I'll use my lucky charms to bake a cake,"
said Layla. "The most delicious cake ever!"

So, Layla hurried home.
She couldn't wait to get started.

Layla went to her kitchen and found her **lucky** cup to measure out the ingredients.

She stirred it all together with her **lucky** spoon.

Then she put it in the oven for three hours.
(Layla's **lucky** number.)

But when she took it out...

it **didn't** look delicious at all!

Layla felt very sad.
How can a lucky ladybug
be this **unlucky**?

Then she noticed a delicious smell

wafting through the window.

Layla followed
the smell
right to…

...Bella's kitchen.

There were melting mud brownies,
pollen pop cakes, and even toadstool tarts!

"My lucky charms aren't lucky any more.
All I've baked is one big mess!" said Layla sadly.

"Don't worry, Layla," they said. "It's not your
lucky charms that help you succeed.
Your achievements come from **you**!"

"Winning the race on sports day showed that your hard work and training paid off!" said Bella.

"Getting a good grade on your spelling test proves that trying your best got results!" said William.

"And your flowers grew so tall because you cared for them and watered them every day!" said Eddie.

Layla realized that she didn't need her
lucky charms after all.

And with a little help from her friends,
Layla baked…

the most **delicious** cake ever!